A Richard Jackson Book

𝒜 ATHENEUM BOOKS FOR YOUNG READERS
New York London Toronto Sydney New Delhi

In the City

Chris Raschka

ATHENEUM BOOKS FOR YOUNG READERS
An imprint of Simon & Schuster Children's Publishing Division
1230 Avenue of the Americas, New York, New York 10020
Copyright © 2020 by Chris Raschka
ATHENEUM BOOKS FOR YOUNG READERS is a registered trademark of Simon & Schuster, Inc.
Atheneum logo is a trademark of Simon & Schuster, Inc.
For information about special discounts for bulk purchases, please contact
Simon & Schuster Special Sales at 1-866-506-1949 or business@simonandschuster.com.
The Simon & Schuster Speakers Bureau can bring authors to your live event.
For more information or to book an event, contact the Simon & Schuster Speakers
Bureau at 1-866-248-3049 or visit our website at www.simonspeakers.com.
Book design by Debra Sfetsios-Conover
The text for this book was set in Eatwell.
The illustrations for this book were rendered in ink and watercolor.
Manufactured in China
0720 SCP
First Edition
10 9 8 7 6 5 4 3 2 1
Library of Congress Cataloging-in-Publication Data
Names: Raschka, Christopher, author, illustrator.
Title: In the city / Chris Raschka.
Description: First edition. | New York : Atheneum Books for Young Readers, [2020] |
"A Richard Jackson book." | Summary: Illustrations and rhyming text celebrate pigeons as colorful,
chatty denizens of the city. Identifiers: LCCN 2019022633 | ISBN 9781481486279 (hardback) |
ISBN 9781481486286 (eBook)
Subjects: CYAC: Stories in rhyme. | Pigeons—Fiction. | City and town life—Fiction. |
Friendship—Fiction.
Classification: LCC PZ8.3.R1768 In 2020 | DDC [E]—dc23
LC record available at https://lccn.loc.gov/2019022633

For
Lydie

IN THE CITY,

tall and good,

over every

neighborhood,

sometimes early, often late,

(doesn't matter what the date)

if you tilt your head up high
you will see the pigeons fly.

Where do friends come from?

Loo loo, loo loo.
Coo coo, coo coo.

Watch them in their tumbling flocks

soaring past the courthouse clock,

circling round apartment towers

even during summer showers.

Clouds and treetops are their homes,
airy houses all their own.

Could a friend be waiting for me?
Too hoo, too hoo.
Coo coo, coo coo.

On a statue they now settle,

chatting on a man of metal.

Oops, they've scattered to the sidewalk

—how they squabble, how they do talk—

finding yesterday's old bagels
underneath the picnic tables.

Perhaps I'll meet my friend today.
Yoo hoo, yoo hoo.
Coo coo, coo coo.

Now we see them one for one—

one is gray and one is brown.

This one has a bluish head.

His or hers is white instead.

Look! The colors on their necks

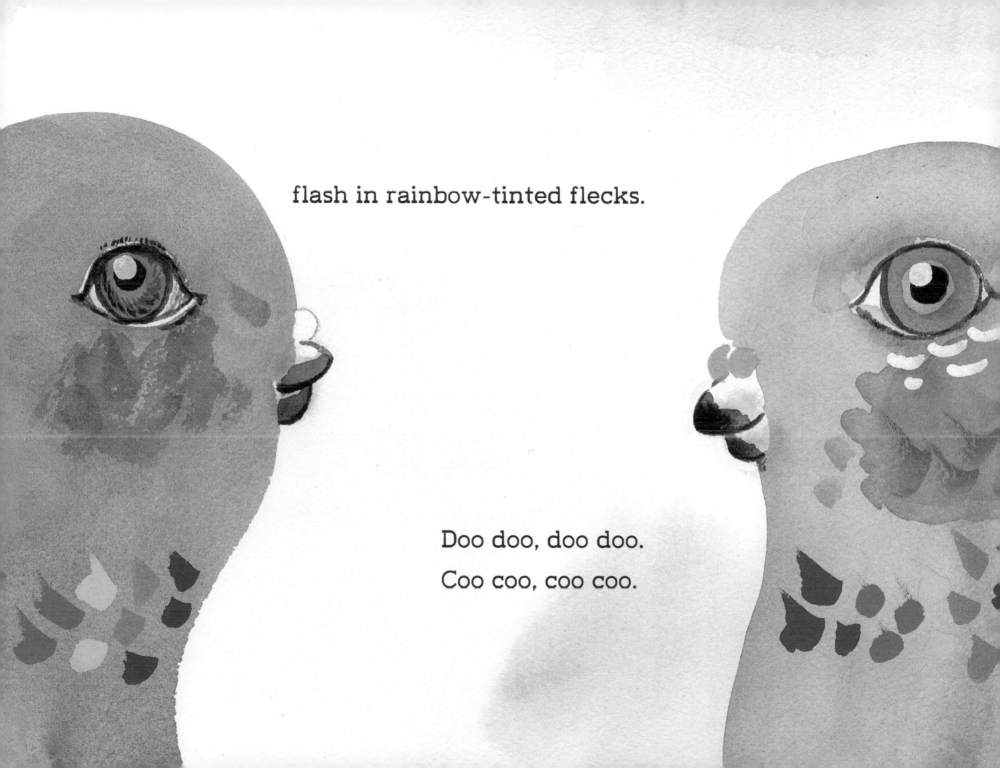

flash in rainbow-tinted flecks.

Doo doo, doo doo.
Coo coo, coo coo.

How do two friends find each other?

Why choose this one, not another?

Are two friends just meant to be—

I for you

and you for me?

I suppose it's in the air.
All my answers are up there.

Now I've found a friend forever.

Noo noo, doo doo.
Coo coo, coo coo.